Also by Heather Grovet

Ready to Ride Series
Zippitty Do Dah

Good as Gold

More titles coming!

Other books by Heather Grovet
Beanie: The Horse That Wasn't a Horse

Marvelous Mark and His No-good Dog

Petunia the Ugly Pug

Prince: The Persnickety Pony That Didn't Like Grown-ups

Prince Prances Again

Sarah Lee and a Mule Named Maybe

What's Wrong With Rusty?

A PERFECT STAR

Heather Grovet

Series Book One

READY TO RIDE SERIES

Pacific Press® Publishing Association
Nampa, Idaho
Oshawa, Ontario, Canada
www.pacificpress.com

Copyright 2007 by
Pacific Press® Publishing Association
Printed in the United States of America
All rights reserved

Book design by Gerald Lee Monks
Cover photo/illustration © Mary Bausman

Additional copies of this book are available by calling
toll-free 1-800-765-6955 or by
visiting http://www.adventistbookcenter.com.

Library of Congress Cataloging-in-Publication Data

Grovet, Heather, 1963-
A perfect star
p. cm. — (Ready to ride ; bk. 1)
Summary: Kendra, Megan, and Ruth-Ann, three
friends who each have ponies, form the Ready to Ride
club and enter competitions. But when Kendra receives
a gift of an English saddle, she must learn to be patient
with herself and others who try to help her.
ISBN 13: 978-0-8163-2164-3
ISBN 10: 0–8163–2164-7
[1. Ponies. 2. Friendship. 3. Christian life. 4. Patience.]
I. Title.

PZ7.G931825Pd 2007
dc22   2006052757

07 08 09 10 11 • 5 4 3 2 1

Dedication

To my friend Rosie, who has the perfect gift—the gift of kindness!

About this series . . .

R²R
READY TO RIDE SERIES

Meet three friends, Kendra, Ruth-Ann, and Megan, and their ponies, Star, Zipper, and Blondie. In this first book, they form the Ready to Ride Club. Each girl plans to become a better rider through horse training and entering shows, and each of them learns about God's love and care for them as they do it. Each book in the series will feature the adventures of one of the girls. Watch for more Ready to Ride stories as they come to your Adventist Book Center.

Contents

The Birthday Present

"It's such an enormous box!" Kendra Rawling exclaimed. "But what could be in it?" Kendra's two best friends, Megan Lewis and Ruth-Ann Chow, grinned back at Kendra and wiggled closer.

Kendra had celebrated her tenth birthday the week before, and she wasn't expecting any more presents. Just that morning, a huge package addressed to Kendra had appeared at the post office. The return address showed that it was from Kendra's Aunt Connie, who lived in Ontario, Canada, far away from the Rawlings' home in Alberta, Canada.

"Maybe it's just a small present wrapped up in that big box to trick you," Ruth-Ann guessed. "My older brother did that last Christmas. He wrapped this great big present and put it under the tree for me, but when I opened it, there was nothing but lots of newspaper inside. And under the newspaper there was just a tiny box holding a key chain."

"It was a nice key chain," Megan said.

Ruth-Ann nodded. "It had a horse on it," she remembered, "so it was nice. But it was still a trick."

"I don't think Aunt Connie's tricking anyone," Mrs. Rawling said with a smile. She passed Kendra a pair of scissors so she could cut the tape that circled the big box.

"And it's too heavy to be only newspaper," Mr. Rawling agreed. "I nearly had a heart attack carrying it into the house!"

"Maybe Aunt Connie's sending me a new horse!" Kendra said. Her fingers fumbled as she hurried to snip through the tape.

"A new horse!" Mr. Rawling groaned. "One horse is enough, more than enough!"

"Star isn't a horse," Kendra said. "She's a Welsh pony."

"She's still enough," Mr. Rawling said.

Everyone's eyes were fastened on the box as Kendra finally removed the last of the sticky tape. With eager fingers she pulled open the flaps of the heavy cardboard with a pop.

The girls peered excitedly into the box.

Something large and dark in color poked out from a pile of bright tissue paper. Kendra reached inside and pushed the paper back. She felt something smooth and sleek, and she smelled a wonderful smell.

"It smells like . . ."

"Leather!" Megan exclaimed.

Inside the box was an English saddle. It was perfectly made of smooth brown leather. The top of the saddle was a deep acorn color, and the bottom of the saddle was made of thinner leather in a light golden tone. Lying loose under the saddle were two leather straps, a pair of silver stirrups, a sleek brown girth, and a wooly English saddle pad.

"I can't believe it!" Kendra shrieked. "I've always wanted to ride English!"

"Me too!" Megan said.

"Me three!" Ruth-Ann agreed.

"How did Aunt Connie know I wanted an English saddle?" Kendra asked, turning to her mother.

Mrs. Rawling reached into the bottom of the box and pulled out an envelope Kendra had missed in all the excitement. "Maybe this will explain everything," she said, handing it to Kendra. The girl ripped open the envelope and read aloud.

"Happy Birthday, dear Kendra!

"This was my saddle when your mother and I were about your age. We made ourselves a riding club called The Happy Riders, and I used the saddle almost every day. I've kept it in my basement all these years, even though I don't own a horse anymore. Now I'm giving it to you so you can learn to ride English. I hope you have as much fun with it as I did!

"I took the saddle to my local tack shop, and they examined everything to make certain it was ready to be used again. I hope the girth is the correct size for Star. The man at the saddle shop assured me that it would fit a small pony. Have fun!

"Love, Aunt Connie.

"P.S. Make sure you wear a helmet when you jump. OK? Because God gives us only one brain, and you need to keep it safe!"

15

"You can learn how to jump!" Ruth-Ann exclaimed. "I think Star will be a wonderful jumper."

"Star's a runt," Mr. Rawling said. "A shrimp. She's too small to jump."

"Dad!"

"She's teeny tiny," Mr. Rawling continued. "Itsy bitsy. Pint-sized. Petite. Almost microscopic!"

"George, when it comes to jumping, size doesn't matter very much," Mrs. Rawling said to her husband. "Welsh ponies are often wonderful jumpers. When Connie and I were teenagers we belonged to a real pony club. And a girl there had a gray Welsh pony almost the same size as Star. That pony could easily out-jump all the bigger horses in the club."

Kendra closed her eyes for a moment. She could picture herself riding Star at a horse show. Star's long white mane would be banded into neat little braids, and the new saddle and pad would fit perfectly. Kendra would wear a tight-fitting pair of breeches and high black boots. Maybe her parents would buy her a proper show jacket, and of course there'd be a trim black-velvet helmet perched on her head.

In Kendra's imagination she could already hear the crowd applauding as the loudspeaker announced the winners. *"And in first place in the jumping class are Kendra Rawling and her pony, A Perfect Star!"*

Kendra's Perfect Star

"Star!" Kendra called. "Come here." The white pony had been grazing the tender summer grass nearby, but when she heard Kendra's voice, she lifted her head. In a moment Star trotted over, politely took an alfalfa cube, and allowed herself to be haltered.

Sometimes I can hardly believe that God gave me such a beautiful pony! Kendra thought. Star was small but built more like a miniature Arabian than a pony. She was snow white and had a long flowing mane and tail. Of course, Kendra knew she would love Star even if she weren't so pretty. How could anyone not love Star? She was well trained and obedient and friendly.

"Your name is just right for you," Kendra said. "Because you're always perfect. You're A Perfect Star." The pony blinked her big brown eyes in agreement.

Kendra's older sister, Nicole, had owned Star first. Back then the pony had been a dappled gray color, but as she grew older, her coat had slowly lightened. Kendra had seen photos of Nicole and Star together, and you could tell that the mare once had a large white star on her gray forehead, and three high white stockings. Now her entire coat was the same pure white as the star and stockings, causing people to wonder about her name.

"Star is part of her registered name," Kendra would explain to those who asked. "A Perfect Star." Mr. Rawling sometimes called the pony "No-Star" or "Starless." But Kendra didn't mind, because she knew that Star was special, even if she did have a name that didn't make sense to others.

"You're going to be a wonderful English horse," Kendra said, tying the pony to the hitching post. "And you aren't too small. You're just the right size for me!" Even though Kendra was in a hurry to try the new English saddle, she still took time to brush Star thoroughly. "I don't want any dirt to hurt your back," she told the pony. She also used a hoof pick to clean out Star's black hooves.

When the pony's coat looked spotless, Kendra lifted the new saddle and pad and slipped them onto Star's back. Kendra couldn't believe how much lighter the English saddle was than her old Western saddle! The new girth was very different from her old one, but Kendra managed to get it fastened.

The stirrups were another thing altogether.

First the silver stirrups had to be slid onto the stirrup leathers. Then each leather hooked onto a metal post under a flap on both sides of the saddle. Kendra's mother had demonstrated how to do it the night before and had offered to help assemble it, but Kendra had decided she could do it herself. Now she wasn't so certain.

It took Kendra a long time and a lot of effort before she finally got the stirrups and leathers into place. She was just slipping the bridle over Star's ears when she heard a familiar *clip-clop* coming down the lane. Star raised her head and nickered.

Fair-haired Megan was in the lead as usual, riding her half-Morgan pony, Blondie. Blondie was palomino, and larger than Star. Her mane was almost exactly the same color as Megan's curly hair.

Blondie and Megan were alike in other ways too. Both of them were always in a rush, wanting to be the first to try something new. Even now Blondie appeared in a hurry, swishing her creamy tail impatiently, and Megan was standing up in her Western stirrups as though trying to make the pony walk faster.

Ruth-Ann and Zipper were quite a distance behind Megan and Blondie, but neither appeared worried as they ambled down the lane. Ruth-Ann was ten years old, but she was taller than Kendra and Megan. Her pony, Zipper, was the biggest pony in the group. He was a small sorrel Paint horse and not actually a pony. He had large splotches of white mixed through his reddish brown hair. Some of his mane was white, and some of it was brown. His face was white except for two perfect sorrel rings around his eyes, which looked a little like glasses.

Zipper was quiet and even lazy sometimes, and he had a way of looking shy until you got to know him. Then you learned that Zipper was a tease. The previous year Zipper had used his teeth to untie himself and get free. When the girls found him, he was carefully untying Star as well!

"Hey, slow-poke," Megan called as they got closer. "We thought you'd be galloping around in your new saddle before we got here."

Kendra frowned, feeling a bit grumpy. Her hand stung where she'd scraped skin off one knuckle while trying to force the leather through the metal bar.

"Can Blondie and I try the English saddle when you're finished riding?" Megan asked as she halted nearby. "I think Blondie would be a terrific English horse." Blondie tossed her head in agreement.

"There's no way this girth will fit around Blondie," Kendra said.

"Blondie isn't that fat this year," Megan said, petting her pony's golden shoulder almost apologetically. "I have her on a diet, and she's getting a lot of exercise."

"I didn't say she was fat," Kendra said. She pulled back her long brown hair and slipped on her riding helmet. "But Blondie's larger than Star, and this girth isn't very long. I have it on the second-to-last notch for Star."

Kendra double-checked to make certain the English saddle was still tightly cinched and then grabbed hold of the front of the saddle. She shoved her toe into the stirrup and swung awkwardly into place.

"How does it feel?" Ruth-Ann asked.

Kendra stood up in the stirrups and adjusted herself. "Hmmmm," she said thoughtfully. "I don't know. It feels . . . strange."

English Problems

The seat of the saddle was smooth and comfortable underneath Kendra. But something seemed wrong. The stirrups were twisted and crooked, and Kendra's toes kept slipping out of position.

"Put your boot farther into the stirrup," Ruth-Ann suggested.

Kendra pushed her toe in farther, but now her entire foot seemed to tilt sideways. She wiggled and adjusted things, but it didn't help.

Ruth-Ann and Megan dismounted and raised Kendra's stirrups, but that didn't seem any better. Next they lowered the stirrups a notch, but the problem didn't go away.

"Maybe that's how all English saddles feel," Megan finally said.

"Then they all feel terrible," Kendra grumbled.

"You haven't given it a chance yet," Megan said. "Let's try it in your riding ring."

Kendra nudged Star with her heels and rode slowly down to the arena. Before long the other two girls were trotting and cantering while Kendra continued to have problems. "This is awful," she muttered, trying to force her feet back into the stirrups after they had trotted a few steps. "I can't ride properly today!"

When Kendra looked up after getting her toes back into position, she saw her parents walking toward her. "Hey girls," Mr. Rawling called, waving his hand. "Have you been bucked off any horses lately?"

"Zipper doesn't buck," Ruth-Ann called back. "He thinks bucking would be too much work!"

"I fell off last week," Megan said, pulling her pony to a halt. "But Blondie didn't buck."

Mrs. Rawling looked concerned. "What happened?" she asked.

"I didn't tighten my saddle enough," Megan said. "And when we started to canter the saddle shifted."

"Oh-oh!"

"Blondie's so round the saddle doesn't stay on very well," Megan said. "I tried to jump off before the saddle turned sideways, but I caught my toe on the saddle horn!"

"Were you wearing your helmet?" Mrs. Rawling asked.

"I always wear my helmet," Megan said. "Mom won't let me ride without it." She put her hand on her shiny white helmet and patted it.

"That's good," Mrs. Rawling said. "Just think what could have happened to your head without it."

"My mom bought me a new helmet last week," Ruth-Ann said. "After Megan fell off. Do you like it, Mrs. Rawling?"

"When I was a girl you could buy a riding helmet in any color you wanted, as long as it was black!" Mrs. Rawling said. "Now they make them in every color under the rainbow." Ruth-Ann's short dark hair barely showed beneath the bright pink helmet she wore.

"What about you, Kendra?" Mr. Rawling asked. "Have you fallen out of the new saddle yet?"

"I haven't fallen off," Kendra admitted. "But I'm having big problems. I think the English saddle's broken."

"Broken?" Mrs. Rawling looked puzzled.

"The stirrups twist around, and I can't keep my feet in position," Kendra said. "I think I'll have to go back to my Western saddle."

Mrs. Rawling smiled. "Oh," she said. "Maybe I can help you. Hop off."

"If you're wise, you'll hop off and stay off," Mr. Rawling said. "That will save your head better than any helmet."

Kendra rolled her eyes and slid out of the saddle.

"Here's your problem," Mrs. Rawling said. She lifted the flap of the saddle and unfastened the stirrup leathers.

"Mom!" Kendra exclaimed. "I spent a long time getting those stirrups in place!"

"English saddles have a right and left stirrup," Mrs. Rawling said. "The stirrups are made to naturally twist one direction so you can ride easily."

"Really?"

"Really," Mrs. Rawling said. "And you have your stirrups on the wrong sides. That's causing your problem."

"Horses are causing all your problems!" Mr. Rawling said. "Not the stirrups. That's why you should sell your horse and buy a motorcycle!"

"Dad, would you really want me to buy a motorcycle?" Kendra asked.

"Sure," Mr. Rawling said. "Then I could ride on it with you."

"Who gets to ride in the front and steer the motorcycle?"

"I do," Mr. Rawling said.

"And what would we do with Star?" Kendra asked.

"She's not driving," Mr. Rawling said. "And that's final!"

"Kendra, let me show you how to put these stirrup irons back in place," Mrs. Rawling said, interrupting the pair. She pointed under the flap of the English saddle. "See that little bar there?" she asked.

"I had a terrible time getting the leather under it," Kendra said.

"The bar has a hinge. If you flip it open this way," Mrs. Rawling said and snapped the bar open, "then it's easy to slip the stirrup leather into place."

"I didn't know that," Kendra said.

"Well, now you do," Mrs. Rawling replied. "But you need to make certain that you close the hinge when you're finished, or the stirrup leather could slide right off when you're riding."

"I don't want that to happen," Kendra said. "Even with my helmet."

Kendra remounted. Now her foot slipped effortlessly into the stirrup. The stirrups did not twist or slide backward. Mrs. Rawling showed the girls how to adjust to the proper length of stirrups. "When you're riding English, the iron should hang directly at your ankle bone," she explained.

"How do you know all these things, Mrs. Rawling?" Ruth-Ann asked.

"I taught her everything she knows," Mr. Rawling said.

"George, you've never been on a horse in your entire life!" Mrs. Rawling said. "And sometimes I think you tease too much. What if these poor girls took you seriously?"

"Mr. Rawling's fun!" Megan said. "We like it when he teases us."

"Some dads don't even talk to us," Ruth-Ann said with a grin. "Mr. Rawling is always friendly. And sometimes he's even funny!"

"Sometimes?" Mr. Rawling said. "I'm *always* funny."

"Ha!" Mrs. Rawling replied with a snort. "Anyhow, I learned how to ride English when I was about your age. My sister and I took riding lessons for several years, and later we joined the Bashaw Pony Club. I think it would be a good idea if we found someone to give you some English riding lessons, too, Kendra. There's a new lady in our church who's supposed to be an excellent English rider and trainer."

Kendra shook her head. "I don't want to take lessons," she said. "Star and I like doing things ourselves."

Before long Kendra and Star were trotting and cantering around the riding ring. The saddle felt very comfortable to Kendra now that it was adjusted properly.

I just knew that Star and I were going to do well at English, Kendra thought happily. *God gave me the perfect little pony.* She trotted Star in a figure eight pattern, making the pony bend smoothly. *I guess I won't jump today. But tomorrow I need to make some jumps. Maybe Dad has some boards I can use.*

Ready, Set, Jump!

Kendra hurried down the lane Friday after school. She knew she would have several chores to do before she could ride, and she didn't want to waste any time.

Kendra's parents weren't home from work yet, but a note on the table listed what Kendra needed to do before the sun set that evening. The first chore was to empty the dishwasher. Kendra did that quickly, being careful not to drop the glasses—she'd broken two glasses just the week before—and then looked at the list again.

"Vacuum the rug," the note said. Kendra grabbed the vacuum cleaner and swiftly began to work. This job took a few minutes longer, especially since the Rawling family owned several parakeets that often made an untidy mess of seeds and feathers around their cage. "I think you enjoy throwing bird seed around," Kendra scolded the birds when she'd finished vacuuming. "How would you like it if I dropped food everywhere and left it for you to clean?"

The birds chirped louder. Kendra peered into their tiny food and water dishes. They were both getting low, so she poured bird seed into one bowl and then fetched clean water for the other.

Kendra's last job was to tidy her room.

This was a job that Kendra hated. Why should she make her bed when she was just going to climb back under the covers again in a few hours? But with a sigh

Kendra threw the blankets back into position. The floor was littered with several pairs of dirty socks. Kendra wadded those into a ball and tossed them into the clothes hamper. On her dresser were a withered apple core and two empty cups. *I guess I'm as bad as the birds,* Kendra thought to herself, *leaving crumbs everywhere.* She threw the apple core in the garbage and popped the cups into the empty dishwasher. Then she picked up a pile of horse magazines and stacked them on her bookshelf.

"There," she said. "I'm done." Kendra grabbed her riding boots and pulled them on before rushing outside.

Kendra had once read a horse advertisement that said, "I bet you know a little girl that would rather clean a stall than clean her room!" That was exactly how Kendra felt! So while Kendra hadn't cared about her room, she did care about the horse jumps. She looked very cautiously as she went through a pile of wood stacked behind her father's shop. She avoided any logs that had splinters or sharp spines of wood that could injure Star, finally selecting several pieces long enough for Star to jump but not too heavy for Kendra to handle.

Kendra wasn't certain how tall she should make the jumps. Photos in horse books showed horses jumping very high—even higher than Kendra's head—but she didn't want to start with something that difficult. After some thought, she set up three jumps using the logs and some metal barrels. She set two jumps about waist height and left one only about as tall as her knees. *I can jump it myself,* she thought, *so Star should be able to do it easily. After all, she has four legs, and I have only two!* Then she scurried across the pasture to catch Star.

Star wasn't so sparkling white that day. She had rolled after her last ride, and she was covered with bits of dried mud and straw. Her left hip and shoulder were marked with large green stains.

Kendra sighed as she brushed the pony. The dirt and straw came off fairly easily with a stiff brush, but the grass stains would not budge. The only way to remove the green stains, Kendra decided, would be to wash the pony with warm, soapy water. It would take a long time to do that, since the nearby outdoor tap only produced cold water. Kendra would have to walk back to the house and fill a bucket with warm water there. Then she would find the special horse shampoo and some clean rags and get to work. By the time she was finished Kendra would be as wet as Star. But Kendra wanted to spend the time riding, not bathing a dirty pony. She decided to ride.

"I just finished a library book that talked about gray horses," Kendra told Star. "The book said that gray horses were kept for royalty. Because only a king or queen could afford to hire people to keep their light-colored horses clean!"

Star swished her tail.

"Do I look like a queen to you, Star?" Kendra continued.

There was no answer, of course, since even ponies as smart as Star can't talk. But Kendra hummed while she tacked up Star. Kendra liked to sing, and thinking about being a queen made her remember a song they had sung at church the previous week. Kendra couldn't remember all the words, but it said something about being "a child of a King."

Kendra knew that she was God's child, and God was a King. So perhaps that made her a princess after all!

Star didn't seem nervous about the new jumps, but she was very curious. She insisted they stop and examine everything carefully. *"These things weren't here before,"* she seemed to say as her muzzle sniffled over each jump.

"Are they scary?" Kendra asked. Star bobbed her head and sniffled louder. Then she raised a front foot and pawed at the jump.

"Watch out!" Kendra exclaimed, but it was too late. The log tipped off the barrel and fell on the ground.

"I think you did that on purpose," Kendra said, laughing. She dismounted and moved Star over a step before setting the jump back into position. Then she remounted and squeezed Star into a trot. After riding at a trot and canter for about ten minutes, Kendra halted Star and studied the jumps. *I'll do the smallest jump first,* Kendra decided. *And then the two bigger ones. Maybe I'll even raise them higher after we've jumped a few times.* In no time at all Star and Kendra would be winning ribbons at horse shows!

Kendra had read a lot of books about jumping, so she thought she knew what to do. Star was a Welsh pony, and they were good jumpers. Jumping was going to be fun. The books said it was like flying.

Star Has Ideas of Her Own

Kendra turned Star to face the lowest jump and gathered the reins. Star began to trot briskly. As they neared the jump, Kendra pushed Star into a canter.

But Star hadn't realized that she was going to do something new. She obediently cantered forward until the small jump was almost directly in front of them. Suddenly Star tossed her head and shied sideways, barely avoiding the jump. Kendra had to grab the pony's long mane to keep from tumbling off.

Star snorted loudly. *"Wow!"* She seemed

to say. *"Did you see how I almost ran into that thing? We've got to be careful or some-one could get hurt!"*

"Star!" Kendra scolded. "Pay attention! We're going to jump."

The pair circled the riding ring again and then turned back toward the jump. But this time Star was prepared.

Star did not want to go over the jump. In fact, she did not want to go anywhere near the jump. She pranced to the left, and then to the right, snorting constantly. Kendra had to pull on the reins to try to keep the pony in line, and when the jump was directly in front of them, the pony still managed to somehow avoid the entire thing.

Now Kendra was upset. "Any horse could jump that tiny thing!" Kendra yelled. "Even a little grasshopper could jump over it!" She gave the mare a firm kick with her heels.

Star broke into a gallop. She circled the ring twice before Kendra was able to slow her down. "OK," Kendra said through gritted teeth. "We'll trot over the jump if we can't canter over it."

Star remained tense and nervous even when they were trotting. *"I don't like this one bit!"* the pony seemed to say. Kendra didn't care. She pointed Star firmly toward the jump.

Star tried to shy to the left, but Kendra pulled on the right rein. Star tried to escape to the right, but Kendra's other rein corrected her. Finally they were straight in front of the jump. Star tried to stop, but Kendra wouldn't allow her to quit.

Star paused, and then at the last second she sprang forward. Kendra almost lost her balance at the pony's sudden move, and she accidentally jerked on Star's reins. The pony didn't stop, but instead of jumping *over* the jump, she crashed right *into* the jump!

The log fell off the barrel and hit the ground with a thud. One of the barrels teetered back and forth and then fell onto its side with a loud crash. Star pinned her ears and spun away.

Kendra didn't know what to do next. Star hated jumping. And it had looked like so much fun in books.

Maybe Star wasn't so perfect after all.

Kendra dismounted and led the pony out of the ring. As soon as they were away from the jumps, Star began to relax. Soon the pony's head lowered. She took a deep breath and shook her head, making her long white mane flip back and forth.

Kendra did not feel very relaxed. Instead she felt frustrated. She tied Star to the hitching post and loosened the girth, sliding off the new saddle and pad. Then she took a plastic currycomb and began to brush the damp sweat marks on Star's back.

What did I do wrong? Kendra asked herself. She thought about her ride in the ring, and how terrible Star had acted. Had it been Star's fault, or her own?

Kendra wished that her older sister, Nicole, was home. Nicole had ridden Star for years and would give her good advice. But now Nicole was attending college far away, and she couldn't be any help at all.

Three Talents and Gifts

On Saturday morning the Rawling family picked Megan up for church. "Is your sister coming with us today?" Mrs. Rawling asked Megan.

Megan shook her head. Her parents never attended church, and her older sister only came occasionally.

"What about your horse?" Mr. Rawling asked, putting the van into gear. "Is she coming?"

Megan laughed. "Blondie thought she'd stay home this morning," she said. "She heard Saturday was supposed to be a day of rest, so she thought she'd do some resting!" Kendra smiled weakly. Today nothing seemed very funny.

Ruth-Ann was waiting for the two girls on the church's front steps. "Look at my new church clothes," she said, twirling around to show off her new skirt and top. "My mom said that she thought of me as soon as she saw them. Aren't they perfect?"

Kendra normally wasn't very interested in clothes, but she had to admit that Ruth-Ann's bright outfit was ideal for her. The pink shirt had a picture of a pair of Paint horses galloping across a colorful field of flowers.

"Why don't we ever ride across a field like that?" Megan asked.

"Because my shirt's just a picture and not real life!" Ruth-Ann said. "I don't think Zipper would even want to gallop across the flowers; he'd probably rather stop and eat them!"

"Nothing's as good as it looks in pictures," Kendra agreed. She couldn't help remembering all the books she'd read about jumping and what a terrible job Star had done when they'd tried it themselves.

The other girls looked at Kendra, wondering why she sounded so gloomy. "We could go for a trail ride at your place," Megan offered. "Even if we can't ride in a field of flowers."

"I can't ride tomorrow," Ruth-Ann said, opening the church door. "It's my little brother's birthday, and the grandparents are all coming over for cake and ice cream."

Kendra sighed. "I don't feel like riding anyhow," she said.

"What?" Ruth-Ann stopped so quickly the other girls bumped into her. "Something must be wrong with you, Kendra Rawling! You're always ready to ride!"

"Something is wrong," Kendra said. In a few moments she had told her friends the story of Star spooking at the little jump and finally crashing into it.

"Well," Megan said when the story was finished, "I'm coming over tomorrow to help you solve this problem. I'm sure Star can learn to jump!"

Sabbath School was just starting when the girls made it to the Junior classroom. Their teacher, Mrs. Campbell, was handing out blank pieces of paper to the children.

"Today we're talking about gifts and talents," Mrs. Campbell said. "Some of us have talents that are easy to recognize. But some of us have talents that are harder to see. Please write down everyone's name on your piece of paper."

There were only six children in juniors, and Kendra quickly wrote down their names. There was Ruth-Ann, Megan, and herself, of course, and three other children.

"Now, I want you to think for a few minutes about the people on your list. Each of them has gifts and talents from God."

One of the boys groaned. "Girls don't have any talents," he said.

Mrs. Campbell frowned, and the boy stopped talking.

"God gives everyone gifts and talents," Mrs. Campbell repeated. "These talents are to be used to help the church and others around us. Please put the numbers one to three by each person's name, and then write down the talents they have."

Ruth-Ann raised her hand. "Do we write down our own talents too?" she asked.

Mrs. Campbell nodded her head. "Yes," she said. "Write down three talents for yourself."

Kendra started with her friends first. It was easy to think of talents for Ruth-Ann and Megan. She wrote

Ruth-Ann:
1. Is an excellent artist.
2. Gets good grades in school, especially in math.
3. Is a hard worker.

Megan:
1. Does really well at all sports.
2. Is a good actor.
3. Doesn't get nervous when she has to speak in public.

It took her a bit longer to think of talents for the three other children, because she didn't know them as well. But the hardest part was naming her own talents. Twice Kendra wrote something and then erased it before thinking again. Finally she came up with three talents for herself.

Kendra:
 1. I have a nice singing voice.
 2. I can play the piano.
 3. I can read better than most kids my
    age.

When everyone was finished, they handed the papers to Mrs. Campbell. The teacher then wrote each student's name and talents on the blackboard.

Everyone agreed that Ruth-Ann was a good artist. Several other people had mentioned that she was great at math. But then there were different talents that Kendra hadn't thought of. Someone mentioned that Ruth-Ann told funny jokes. Someone else said Ruth-Ann was a good teacher because she could help them understand difficult math problems even better than their real school teacher.

Kendra felt shy when Mrs. Campbell wrote her name on the bulletin board. What if no one thought she had any talents?

But Mrs. Campbell wrote a long list of talents by her name. Almost everyone agreed that Kendra was an excellent singer and piano player. Someone—Kendra felt certain it was Megan—had written down that she was a good horse trainer. And then there were talents that Kendra had never really thought about before.

- Kendra is nice to little kids
- She's a good sport
- She doesn't gossip
- She'll share with others

When they were all finished, Kendra raised her hand. "Some of those things don't sound like talents or gifts," she said.

"Yeah," Ruth-Ann agreed. "Why would God care if someone is funny or not? Or a good sport?"

Mrs. Campbell smiled. "God created us all different," the teacher said. "Some people have gifts that are easy to see, such as being an artist or a musician or a writer. It's easy to tell their talents, because they are public talents. But some of our gifts are more private and personal, like the gift of humor, or patience, or kindness. Sometimes those gifts don't seem important to us, but I think they can be the most important gifts of all in God's eyes."

Megan raised her hand slowly. "I wish I had different gifts," she said.

"What gift would you like?" Mrs. Campbell asked.

"I want to be a singer when I grow up," Megan said. "I've taken voice lessons for two years, and I still don't sound that great when I sing. Kendra takes lessons from the same teacher, and she sings wonder-fully. Why is that?"

"I'd like to be a better musician, too," Mrs. Campbell agreed. "But God made us all different. He has a special purpose for each of us. He knows what talents and gifts we need to help people around us. Maybe God wants you to be a singer. But maybe He has a different plan for you."

"Is it OK to keep taking voice lessons?" Megan asked.

"Of course," Mrs. Campbell said. "With practice we can improve our skills and learn new ones. What really matters is that we use all our talents for God."

"What if my main talent is horse rid-ing?" Ruth-Ann asked. "How can I use that for God?"

"I'm not sure what God has planned for your life," Mrs. Campbell said, "But I know that all our gifts have a purpose. I would guess that being a good horse rider teaches you to be kind to animals, and patient and hard working. Those are important things."

Mrs. Campbell then said a prayer and dismissed the class.

Kendra was quiet as she walked up the stairs between Ruth-Ann and Megan. She was thinking very seriously about what Mrs. Campbell had said. If she used her horse-riding talents for God, how would she act? Would she be angry at Star when she was being bad? Or would she try to find a better way to solve the problem?

Blondie Tries to Jump

There was a knock on the Rawling front door Sunday afternoon. "There are two lovely blondes here to see you, Kendra," Mr. Rawling called. "But where are the brown-haired ladies?"

Megan giggled. "Do you mean Ruth-Ann, Mr. Rawling?" she asked. She stood near the doorstep, holding Blondie's reins in her hands.

"Of course," Mr. Rawling said. "And Zipper."

"Ruth-Ann's hair is almost black," Megan said. "Not brown. And Zipper's a boy. So they aren't brown-haired ladies!"

"Close enough for me," Mr. Rawling said.

"They're at home," Megan continued. "Ruth-Ann had to stay home for her little brother's birthday party."

Kendra quickly grabbed her coat. "May I take Star for a ride?" she asked.

"Yes, you may," Mrs. Rawling called. "Keep safe and have fun."

"Good luck with that," Mr. Rawling said. "No one has fun riding horses. Now, if you had a motorcycle, it would be different!"

Megan tied Blondie to the hitching post and waited while Kendra caught Star. Then the two girls began to brush the white pony. "I can pick out her hooves for you," Megan offered.

Kendra nodded her head. "Thanks," she said.

Before long Star was ready to be saddled. "Do you think I should ride English or Western?" Kendra asked.

"English, of course," Megan said eagerly. "I want to watch you two jump."

"I thought we'd just go for a trail ride across the pasture," Kendra said.

"We can go for a long trail ride," Megan said. "But first I want to see Star jump."

"We're a disaster," Kendra said with a sigh.

"Maybe it will go better today," Megan said. "Blondie might make Star more relaxed. I know I always feel better with a friend nearby."

Kendra shrugged her shoulders and began to tack up with the English saddle. Megan stood nearby, watching everything with interest. "Maybe I'll get an English saddle of my own," she said. "I told Mom I wanted one for Christmas."

Kendra showed her how to position the pad under the saddle, and how to tighten the new girth. "That doesn't seem too difficult," Megan commented when Star was totally tacked up.

"Saddling English is the easy part," Kendra said. "It's the riding English that I'm having problems with."

"You were riding English really well a few days ago."

"OK," Kendra said. "I guess jumping is the difficult part. But I really wanted to jump. Why have an English saddle if you can't jump?"

Star didn't even want to go into the riding ring. She acted nervous as soon as she walked through the gate, snorting once or twice. *"Watch out, Blondie,"* she seemed to say. *"There's a jump monster here this week."*

Blondie marched briskly around the ring, totally ignoring the new jumps. Her legs moved in a golden blur, and Star had to trot to keep up. "OK," Megan said after they had warmed up the ponies. "Let's see what Star does."

Kendra halted the little mare and patted her neck soothingly. "OK, Star," she said. "If you jump once, we'll quit and go for a nice trail ride." Taking a deep breath she pointed the pony at the smallest jump and put her into a steady trot.

Star trotted halfway across the ring before she realized where they were heading. *"You tricked me! I thought we weren't jumping!"* she seemed to say. She pinned her ears back against her head. Once again Kendra had to concentrate to keep the pony moving in a straight line. Star ducked to the left several steps and then stopped.

Kendra circled the jump and urged the pony forward again.

Again Star stopped, and this time backed up several steps quickly.

"You make me so angry!" Kendra growled. She gripped the reins even tighter, and thumped her heels on Star's sides. Star pranced forward a few steps, hesitated, and then sprang forward over the jump.

This time Star's front feet went over the jump, but her back feet hit the wooden log with a crash! When Kendra was able to halt Star, she turned and saw the narrow log was now broken in two.

"Oh dear," Megan said. "You must have hit that log pretty hard for it to break!"

"I hate jumping," Kendra said. *And sometimes I think I hate Star, too!*

"Would you mind if I try to jump Blondie?" Megan asked slowly.

"Go ahead," Kendra said. "But it's difficult to jump in a Western saddle."

"We'll just jump once," Megan said. She dismounted and pulled the broken pieces of wood out of the way. She took a new log and set it up on the low barrels.

Megan got back in the saddle and nudged Blondie. The little palomino moved into a fast trot and then began to canter toward the jump.

"Be careful," Kendra called.

Blondie sprang into the air and easily made it over the little jump before continuing to canter around the ring.

Megan's face beamed. "That was fun!" she called. "Almost like flying!"

Kendra didn't say anything. She thought Megan wasn't being a lot of help to her right then. If Blondie could jump that easily, why couldn't Star?

Ready
to Ride

It was almost dusk when Megan returned to Kendra's house with Ruth-Ann.

"How was your little brother's birthday party?" Mrs. Rawling asked, meeting the two girls at the door.

"Terrible!" Ruth-Ann groaned. "Mikey smeared cake everywhere! It was on his face and high chair, and even in his hair. And then he screamed when we tried to wash him!"

"Poor Mikey," Megan said.

"Poor Mikey?" Mrs. Rawling asked.

"You should probably say poor Mrs. Lewis!"

"I know," Ruth-Ann said. "Mikey screamed so loud you probably could have heard him from here."

"Maybe Mikey just wanted to save the cake crumbs for later," Mr. Rawling suggested.

"Why would he save cake crumbs?" Kendra asked.

"For a snack, of course," Mr. Rawling said. "What else would you do with cake?"

Megan and Ruth-Ann laughed. Kendra didn't even smile. The three girls walked to Kendra's bedroom. "I know how Mikey feels," Kendra said. She shut her door and flopped over on the bed. "I would like to scream too."

"You don't have any cake on your face!" Ruth-Ann joked.

Kendra frowned. "I think there's something wrong with Star. Blondie can jump perfectly. And Star can't even get near the jump without going crazy."

"What are you going to do?" Ruth-Ann asked.

"I need help solving this problem," Kendra said. "I wish I belonged to a pony club or something. They could give me advice better than any book."

"I have an idea!" Megan said. "Why don't we make our own club?"

"Make a real pony club?" Kendra asked.

"Zipper couldn't belong to a pony club, because he isn't a pony," Ruth-Ann said.

"A pony club is for horses and ponies," Kendra said. "My mom told me that pony clubs started in England, where they sometimes call horses 'ponies.' Don't ask me why. But it isn't for ponies only. So Zipper could belong."

"We couldn't start a real pony club," Megan said. "That would be too difficult, and we'd need grown-up leaders and everything. But wouldn't it be fun to start a riding club of our very own?"

"We could call ourselves the Happy Riders," Ruth-Ann said. "That's what your Aunt Connie's club was called."

"I don't feel like a happy rider right now," Kendra grumbled.

"Well, then we need a different name," Megan said. "All clubs have names."

"How about Iron Creek Riders?" Ruth-Ann suggested. "That would be a good name."

"Boring," Megan said. "Besides, the horse 4-H club calls themselves Iron Creek 4-H. We don't want to be the same."

"Do you have a better idea?" Kendra asked.

"We could call ourselves the Saddle

Riders," Megan suggested. "Or maybe the Saddle Bags!"

"I don't want to be a Saddle Bag!" Ruth-Ann exclaimed. "That sounds awful!"

"That sounds like a name my dad would have thought of," Kendra said.

"That's pretty bad," Megan groaned. "So we'd better think of something else!" The girls were quiet for a moment.

"I have an idea," Kendra said slowly. "We could be the R2R Club."

"R2R?" Ruth-Ann asked. "What's that mean?"

"Ready to Ride," Kendra explained. "It's a perfect name, because we're always ready to ride. And the boys at school wouldn't know what we were talking about when we said we were going to an R2R meeting."

"That's a great idea!" Megan agreed.

Ruth-Ann nodded. "I like it too," she said. "The Ready to Ride Club."

69

"What are we going to do in our club?" Kendra asked.

"Have meetings," Ruth-Ann said. "And we can plan events. Like a horse show—that would be fun!"

"Or maybe we could take the horses on a camping trip!" Megan said. "I've always wanted to go camping with Blondie."

"Or we could learn how to barrel race," Kendra said, beginning to be interested in spite of herself. "Star can't jump, but maybe she could do the barrels."

"Zipper would be an awful barrel racer," Ruth-Ann said. "He doesn't like to go fast."

"The very first thing we should do is solve Star's problem," Megan said. "Real clubs help their members, and we need to help Kendra."

"I don't know if anyone can help me," Kendra sighed.

"Here's what we need to do," Megan continued. She passed three pieces of paper around the room. "Write down why you think Star won't jump."

"You sound just like Mrs. Campbell," Kendra said.

"I liked Mrs. Campbell's idea," Megan said. "And I thought it worked in Sabbath School. Why won't it work for the R2Rs?"

In a few minutes the girls were finished. Kendra read first.

"I'm afraid Star is just being disobedient. I know that she can jump, but she won't. Maybe she's just being a brat. If she's just being bad, then she needs a better rider to make her behave. Maybe I'm not the right rider for Star. Or maybe we shouldn't ride English anymore."

Kendra read her suggestion out loud.

Both Ruth-Ann and Megan shook their heads.

"I don't think Star wants to be disobedient," Megan said. "You've had Star for a long time, and she normally tries to be good. If she was just spoiled, then she wouldn't be so obedient for other things."

"You're an experienced rider," Ruth-Ann said. "And you handle Star well. So there must be something else wrong."

Kendra thought about that. It was true that Star was normally a very well-behaved pony. So there must be more to the problem.

Next Megan read her idea.

"Maybe Star's feet or legs hurt so she can't jump. Maybe she'd be better with horse shoes. Maybe the new saddle pinches her back so she doesn't want to jump. Maybe Kendra needs a different bridle for Star's

mouth. We could talk to a vet about the problem."

When Megan was finished the girls thought for a moment. Finally Kendra spoke up. "I don't think Star's feet or legs hurt. She doesn't mind trotting and cantering if we aren't jumping."

"And she doesn't limp," Ruth-Ann said.

"And she was obedient on our trail ride this afternoon," Megan agreed. "And you used the English saddle and bridle. So that can't be the problem."

They crossed off that idea too.

Finally it was time for Ruth-Ann's suggestion.

"I think Star doesn't know how to jump. At first she was just scared to try something new. Then she finally jumped, but she hit her legs on the board, and that hurt. Now

73

she's even more afraid. We need to find a way to show Star that jumping won't hurt her."

The girls looked at each other. "That makes sense," Kendra said hopefully. "Star could just be scared of the jumps."

"But it's so small!" Megan said. "Kendra didn't ask her to go over a difficult jump. And Blondie jumped it the very first time."

"Weren't you listening to Mrs. Campbell?" Ruth-Ann asked.

"Mrs. Campbell wasn't talking about horses," Kendra said.

"She talked about people," Ruth-Ann said, "but maybe it's the same for horses. Mrs. Campbell said that people have different gifts and strengths because God has different purposes for them. Well, maybe it's the same thing for horses."

"And Mrs. Campbell said it's good to practice things even if they aren't our real talents," Megan said. "We just need to find a different way to teach Star to jump."

"We could put the log flat on the ground and teach Star to walk over it," Ruth-Ann suggested. "Then she could go over the log without hurting herself."

"That's a great idea!" Megan said.

Kendra suddenly felt much better. Her pony wasn't being disobedient. She just hadn't learned how to jump yet. "It's OK," Kendra said. "It doesn't really matter if Star becomes a great jumper. I'll love her anyhow."

"I have one more idea," Ruth-Ann said.

"What?"

"Your mom said you could take English riding lessons. Why don't you do that? Maybe Megan and I could come too."

"But it's fun to do things without help," Kendra said.

"But it would be fun to do lessons together, too," Megan said eagerly. "R2R lessons! Remember, we're always ready to ride!"

Riding Lessons at Last

"My name is Trish Klein," the horse trainer said. She shook hands with Kendra, Megan, and Ruth-Ann. "You can call me Trish." She was a tall, slim woman with long blond hair pulled back in a simple ponytail.

The three girls stood in the arena, holding their ponies' reins. "For our first lesson I'd like each of you to ride alone," Trish said. "That way I can learn more about you and your ponies. OK?"

The three girls nodded.

"Well," Trish said. "Who's first?"

The R2R club members looked at each other. No one said anything.

"Let's not all rush to be first," Trish said with a smile. "Come on, someone's got to be the brave one."

Ruth-Ann and Kendra raised their hands and pointed at Megan. "Megan's the brave one," Ruth-Ann said. "Pick her."

Megan grinned and then smoothly mounted Blondie. "I really want to learn how to ride English," Megan said. "But that's probably silly since I don't even own an English saddle."

"That isn't silly," Trish said. "We'll just have to be creative. I can teach you how to post properly, and how to ride the two-point position. Then when you do buy an English saddle, you'll be prepared."

Trish sent Megan out to the rail and watched carefully as the pair went through their paces. In about ten minutes she called Megan back to the center of the ring.

"You have a very nice pony," Trish said, scratching Blondie's amber-colored neck. "And you both will do well at English. Blondie has a natural headset and a good working trot. And you ride her very well. You have a secure seat and good hands. But I notice that Blondie doesn't bend very easily when you turn, so that's something we need to improve. I want to show you a different way to turn your horse."

Trish set up several markers in the ring and instructed Megan to ride Blondie in a large figure eight around them. "Don't pull your hand to the side, away from you," Trish instructed the girl as they turned to the right. "Instead bring your hand back toward your hip." Blondie almost immediately rounded her back and turned more smoothly.

"Wow!" Megan said. "That felt better."

"Next time I want you to do the same thing with your hands," Trish said. "But this time we're going to have you use your legs differently. Put your left leg back behind the girth, and keep your right one where it is."

"Circles are harder than I realized," Megan said after they made several more loops.

"Yes, they are," Trish agreed. "But look how much smoother Blondie's turning already."

After doing several more exercises Trish held up her hand. "That's enough for one day," she said. "Both of you have already made progress. Let's not overdo things in our first lesson." Trish then motioned to Ruth-Ann and Zipper. "You're next," she said.

Zipper was even lazier than usual, probably because he didn't enjoy working while his friends stood in the center of the ring. Soon Ruth-Ann was huffing and puffing, trying to keep Zipper moving.

"How old is your horse?" Trish asked while Ruth-Ann caught her breath.

"Zipper's five years old," Ruth-Ann said.

"That explains a lot," Trish said. "Zipper is a nice, quiet horse. But since he's only five, he's really just a big kid himself. He hasn't had a lot of formal training."

"I know," Ruth-Ann said. "But he's a really super horse." She reached down and hugged Zipper.

"First we must teach Zipper to respect your legs," Trish said. "Do you own a pair of spurs?"

"No!" Ruth-Ann exclaimed. "Spurs are terrible. They could hurt Zipper."

Trish shook her head. "You can choose to use any tool cruelly," she said. "Zipper's bit could hurt him if you jerked your hands roughly. And spurs could be cruel if you used them roughly."

"But—"

"Ruth-Ann," Trish said, "you can trust me. I love horses, and I would never ask you to do something cruel. We're going to use spurs properly. At first you'll squeeze your legs softly, even if you know that won't work. And then, if Zipper doesn't listen, you're going to kick his sides with your boots firmly. And if that doesn't work, then you are going to use your spurs. Not roughly, but firmly enough that Zipper knows he has to obey."

"Well . . ." Ruth-Ann said, hesitating.

"Is Zipper a stupid horse?" Trish asked. "Or a smart one?"

"He's the only horse I know that can untie his own lead rope," Ruth-Ann said.

"And he can untie the other horses too," Kendra agreed.

"He can open gates with his teeth," Ruth-Ann said. "Once he let himself out of the corral and then opened the door to the chicken coop and let all

Mom's chickens loose. Mom was pretty mad at him!"

"But is that being smart or stupid?" Megan asked with a grin.

"Oh, that's definitely something that only an intelligent horse could do," Trish said. "Zipper's smart enough to get himself into trouble sometimes. He probably can pick up bad habits quickly. But that also means that he's smart enough to learn a lesson quickly too. Ruth-Ann, I think that you'll only have to use the spurs once or twice, and Zipper will become much more obedient."

Ruth-Ann slowly nodded her head. "OK," she said. "I'll try. But you have to help me, Trish."

"Don't worry," Trish said. "I'll be back next week to give you girls another lesson. And we'll keep working so you and your horse can keep improving."

Trish Tells
the Truth

Finally it was Kendra's turn. Star was hesitant at first when they rode near the jumps, but before long she realized they weren't trying to jump and relaxed. Kendra concentrated, trying to remember all the things her mother had taught her about good equitation. She kept her heels down and her shoulders straight.

"Kendra, you are a natural young rider," Trish said after calling the pair into the center of the ring. "And Star is a lovely pony. She has smooth gaits, and she pays attention to your cues. With practice she will be a wonderful English pony."

"She's being good now," Kendra said. "But you should see what happens when I try to get her to jump. It's awful." Kendra explained the whole story and then finished with a huge sigh. "I thought Star would be the perfect English pony," she said sadly. "That's her name, you know. A Perfect Star."

Trish smiled. "Kendra, I know you girls are Christians, so I want to share something with you."

"Is this for Kendra," Ruth-Ann asked, "or all of us?"

"This applies to all of you," Trish said. "The Bible says there isn't a single person in the world who's perfect. Only Jesus was perfect. That's why He had to come to earth to die on the cross and save us from our sins. We all do things wrong sometimes, and we need someone to help us."

"That's true," Ruth-Ann said softly.

"Well," Trish continued. "If no person is perfect, than why would we expect an animal to be perfect?"

"But Star is normally so good," Kendra said.

"Being good isn't the same as being perfect," Trish said. "Star is a good pony, but she still does things wrong sometimes."

"So I should just accept that Star won't jump?" Kendra asked.

"No," Trish said. "Star can improve her jumping."

"But what are we going to do?"

Trish ran her fingers through Star's long mane. "If people take their problems to Jesus and trust Him, they can improve. They might not be perfect, but they can get better," Trish said slowly. "If we're fair and kind to Star, she'll learn to trust us with the jumps, and then she can improve, too. Even if she isn't perfect."

"But why would she be scared of a little jump?" Kendra wondered. "I didn't do anything wrong."

"But what happened to Star *before* you owned her?" Trish asked. "Perhaps she tried to jump before, and something bad happened."

"I never thought about that."

"When I was a kid I tried to jump my pony, Taffy, over a pole resting on two plastic lawn chairs," Trish said. "It seemed like a good idea at the time. The chairs were the right height, and the pole didn't roll accidentally off because the arms of the chair held it in position."

Kendra nodded.

"One day Taffy bumped the pole with his front legs when we tried to jump it. On a real jump the pole normally would just fall on the ground, and no one would be hurt. But this pole couldn't roll off because it was stuck between the chair arms. When Taffy hit the jump, everything fell over with a crash, including us. Taffy toppled onto his knees, and I rolled right over him and onto the hard dirt."

"Were you hurt?" Kendra asked.

"A little," Trish said. "My helmet protected my head, but I ended up with some big bruises on my legs and body. And after that Taffy was afraid to jump."

"Wow!"

"I had to start all over again," Trish said. "I had to teach Taffy that jumping wasn't going to hurt him. Plus I needed to be smart and not put him in a position where something bad could happen again."

"Did it work?" Ruth-Ann asked.

"Yes, it did," Trish said. "Later Taffy and I won a lot of jumping competitions. But I just about ruined everything with that one silly mistake."

"So you don't think Star is just being disobedient?" Kendra asked.

"We need to help Star," Trish said. "And not be mad at her. I don't want you to try to jump Star at all this week, Kendra."

"OK," Kendra agreed.

"Next week we'll start working over ground poles," Trish continued.

"Ground poles?"

"Ground poles are just poles that rest flat on the dirt," Trish said. "We'll teach Star to walk over them, and later trot over them. When she realizes that we're keeping her safe, she'll start to relax. In the future we can raise them just a few inches high, and she can learn to step over them too. Inch by inch we'll go higher, and see how things go from there."

"That was my idea!" Ruth-Ann said. "But I thought it would take a long time to help."

"Sometimes you have to work slowly if you want to make progress," Trish said. "With time we can teach Star that we'll always keep her safe, even when things appear a bit scary."

"Maybe I shouldn't jump Blondie either until we do some jumping lessons," Megan said. "I don't want to do anything that would hurt her."

"That's a good idea," Trish agreed. "And girls, there's another lesson in this story. Star needs to learn to trust us, and we need to learn to trust God. He will take care of us even when things seem to be going wrong."

Trish then said Goodbye to the girls and walked over to the Rawling house to talk to Kendra's parents. The three girls began to untack their ponies.

"That was a great lesson," Megan said.

"I learned a lot," Kendra agreed as she worked a snarl out of Star's thick tail.

"I thought I knew how to ride," Megan said. "But I was making a lot of mistakes. Blondie is bending and turning better after one lesson with Trish. I always thought the way she turned poorly was all her fault, but now I see that I was doing things wrong too."

"Wait until you see what Zipper's going to learn," Ruth-Ann said. "I'm going to practice a lot this week."

"You can ride in our ring anytime you want," Kendra said, "and then we can practice together."

"I'm so glad we have an R2R Club," Ruth-Ann said. "And riding lessons. With Trish's help we solved our first real problem."

Kendra smiled and closed her eyes for a moment. *Thank You, God,* she prayed, resting her face on Star's soft neck. *I'm so glad I have Star, even if she isn't always perfect. And thank You for Trish. And thanks*

A PERFECT STAR

for Megan and Ruth-Ann, my R2R friends. They really helped me today. Help me to always use my talents and gifts to help others too.

R²R

Words of Advice About Owning a Pony

Wouldn't it be wonderful to have a horse or pony like Star?

I have four horses and a miniature pony, and while they are all really nice animals, none of them are perfect. But they are well trained, and I work hard to keep them from learning bad habits.

Before you start searching for a pony or horse of your own, you and your family need to put in a lot of time, thought, and prayer into your decision. Are you all *really* prepared for the work, time, and money that go into owning a horse? If not, you might do better to rent or borrow a horse at a nearby stable.

Buying the perfect kid's horse is very difficult. Ask God to help you make good choices. Ask God to open your eyes so you can turn away from the "beautiful, flashy" horses and look at the less fancy but more sensible ones. Ask God to help you to be patient as you hunt for the right horse. And ask God to keep you safe when you ride—just as you need Him to help you with all your activities.

The ideal kid's horse is well trained. He turns and stops and moves forward quietly. He doesn't get impatient with little hands and feet as you learn to ride. He stands quietly when he's brushed and saddled. He isn't likely to shy or spook, and he doesn't like to rush around all the time. Of course, even a good kid's horse can have bad days, but they should have more quiet days than silly ones.

Kid's horses come in a wide variety of sizes and shapes. Don't pay much attention to their color or breed. Instead choose a well-trained, older horse or pony that's used to children.

Then you can have fun like Kendra, Megan, and Ruth-Ann.

And like me, too.

Happy Trails!
Heather Grovet

Want more horse stories? You'll enjoy these also.

The Sonrise Farm Series

Based on true stories, *Katy Pistole's* Sonrise Farm series about Jenny Thomas and her Palomino mare, Sunny, teaches children about horses and God's redeeming grace. (ages 11–13) Paperback, 128 pages each. US$7.99 each.

Book 1 **The Palomino**
Jenny Thomas has her heart set on one thing—a golden Palomino all her own. Her daring rescue of an abused horse at an auction begins an enduring friendship with Sunny. 0-8163-1863-8

Book 2 **Stolen Gold**
Book two in the series finds Sunny in the clutches of an abusive former owner who wants to collect insurance money on the Palomino and her colt. 0-8163-1882-4

Book 3 **Flying High**
A record-breaking jump, Sunny's reputation, and Jenny's relationship with God are all at stake when Jenny and her Palomino champion come face to face with their old enemy. 0-8163-1942-1

Book 4 **Morning Glory**
Sunny's foal is born, but an evil plan from Jenny's old enemy, Vanessa DuBois, threatens all of them. But God has a plan to restore their lives. 0-8163-2036-5

Order from your ABC by calling **1-800-765-6955**, or get online and shop our virtual store at **http://www.Adventist BookCenter.com.**
- Read a chapter from your favorite book
- Order online
- Sign up for e-mail notices on new products

Prices subject to change without notice.